Gopher Up Your Sleeve

by **Tony Johnston**

illustrated by **Trip Park**

For Jenny
—T. J.

To my little critters, Sumner, Hampton, and Lawson
—T. P.

Text © 2002 by Tony Johnston
Illustrations © 2002 by Trip Park
All rights reserved.

"Bad Decision," "Boing," "Jellyfish Walk," and "Frog Eggs" were previously published in
I'm Gonna Tell Mama I Want an Iguana, (G. P. Putnam's Sons, NY), © 1990 by Tony Johnston.
"Caterpillar" was previously published in *Small Talk: A Book of Short Poems*,
(Harcourt Brace & Company, NY), © 1995 by Tony Johnston.

www.northlandpub.com

The illustrations were rendered digitally on a Macintosh using Fractal Design's Painter
The text type was set in Formata Light
The display type was set in Blue Century
Designed by Chantelle Call
Edited by Aimee Jackson
Production supervised by Donna Boyd

Composed in the United States of America
Printed in Hong Kong

01 02 03 04 05   5 4 3 2 1

Library of Congress Cataloging-in-Publication Data
Johnston, Tony
Gopher up your sleeve / by Tony Johnston; illustrated by Trip Park.
p. cm.
Summary: Brief, humorous rhymes describe animals both ordinary and unusual, including a rooster, a javelina, and a python.
ISBN 0-87358-794-4
[1.Animals—Fiction. 2. Stories in rhyme.] I. Park, Trip, ill. II.Title.
PZ8.3.J639 Go 2001

[E]—dc21   2001019773

Small Rodent Chant

(for Jenny)

Eve, Eve,
I believe
there's a gopher
up your sleeve.

Claire, Claire,
I don't care.
There's a hamster
in *your* hair!

Maybe a Booby

In a nest of dust, there appears to be
a barefoot, blue-foot booby.

If I gain her trust, I could glimpse—maybe—
her blue-foot booby baby.

Parrot and Leaf

A parrot's like a green leaf walking.

The difference is the parrot's squawking.

Two of a Kind

They met upon a moonlight night.
And both had suckers big as dimes.
But one was fat and one was flat,
a problem at the best of times.
Still, things worked out. 'Twas love on sight
for the octopus and the bathtub mat.

Crab

Crab O crab, I love you so,
        your salty smell, your crusty shell,
your clamplike claws that pinch so well.
        I love you, crab, but *please* let go!

Jellyfish Walk

When jellyfish go walking,
there isn't any talking
or giggling.
There's phlup,
          phlup,
                   phlup.

When jellyfish are stopping,
there's plenty of slip-slopping
and jiggling
to stop,
         stop,
               stop.

Storm Song

Rooty-tooty-too.
The sky is clear and blue.
Seven silly shrimps
canoeing in the stew.

Rooty-tooty-tall.
Here comes a monster squall!
Seven silly shrimps
white-water down the hall.

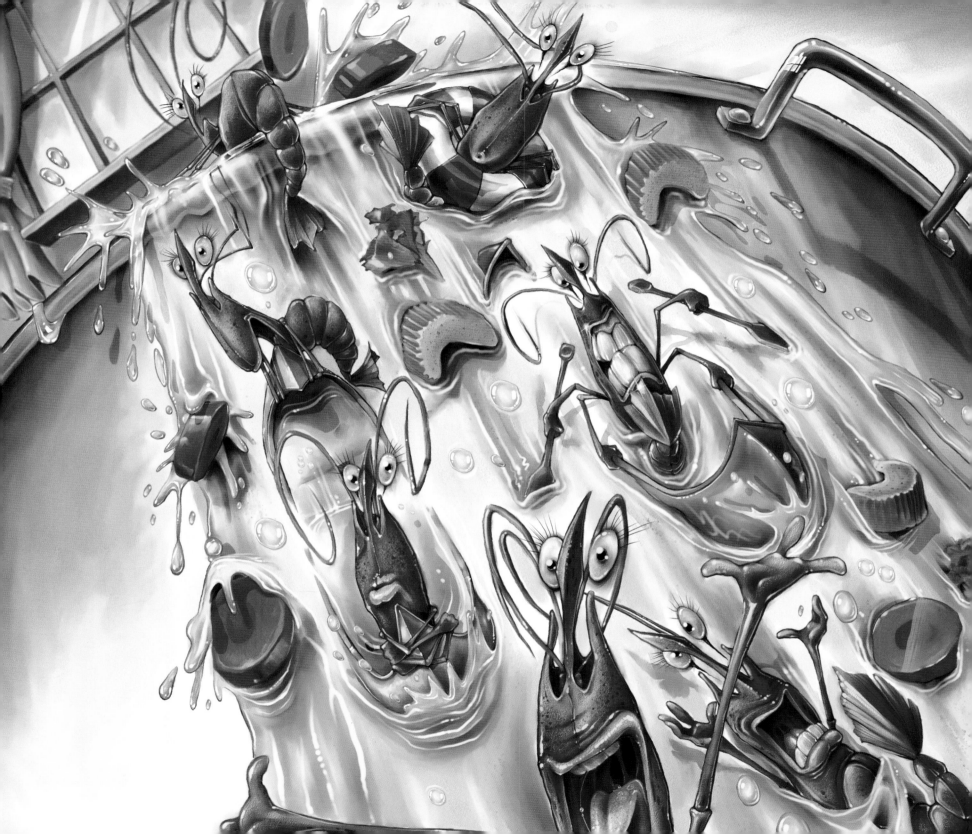

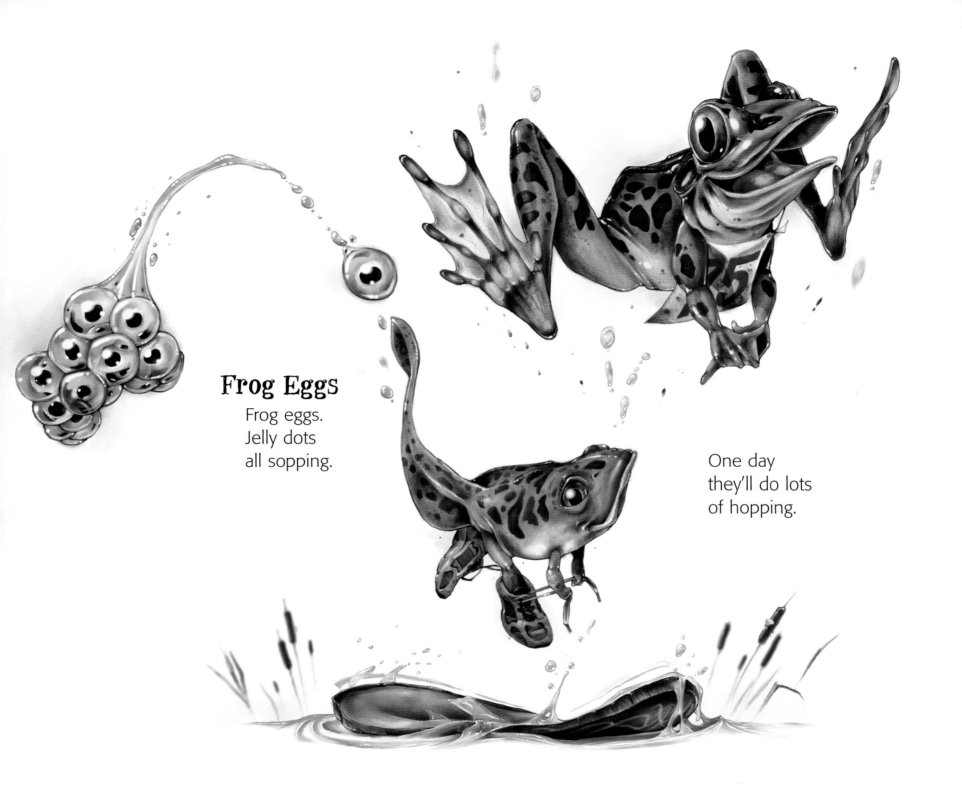

Frog Eggs

Frog eggs.
Jelly dots
all sopping.

One day
they'll do lots
of hopping.

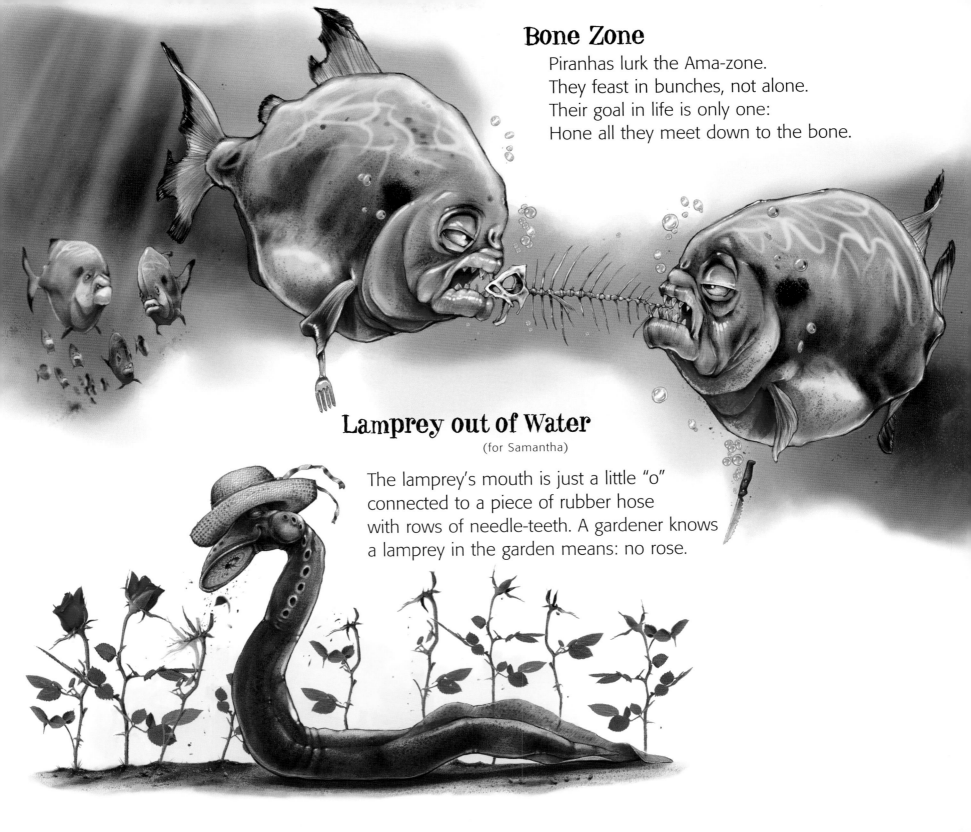

Bone Zone

Piranhas lurk the Ama-zone.
They feast in bunches, not alone.
Their goal in life is only one:
Hone all they meet down to the bone.

Lamprey out of Water

(for Samantha)

The lamprey's mouth is just a little "o"
connected to a piece of rubber hose
with rows of needle-teeth. A gardener knows
a lamprey in the garden means: no rose.

Bzzzzzzzzzzz

This time of year my head begins to hum.
I feel as though I live inside a drum.
My work is numbing—long and noisy hours.
(The pay won't buy a crumb—it's all in flowers.)
I'd like to take a trip to somewhere still.
(When winter comes again maybe I will.)
Now spring is tuning up, and she needs me
to keep things humming. I'm the buzz of bees.

Pill Bug

When life is sweet,
on all my feet
I stroll, I stroll.

Danger in sight,
I ball-up tight.
I roll! I roll!

Caterpillar

Caterpillar. Bulgy. Brown.
Creeping up the rose.
Soon you will be beautiful
In your party clothes.

Manatee

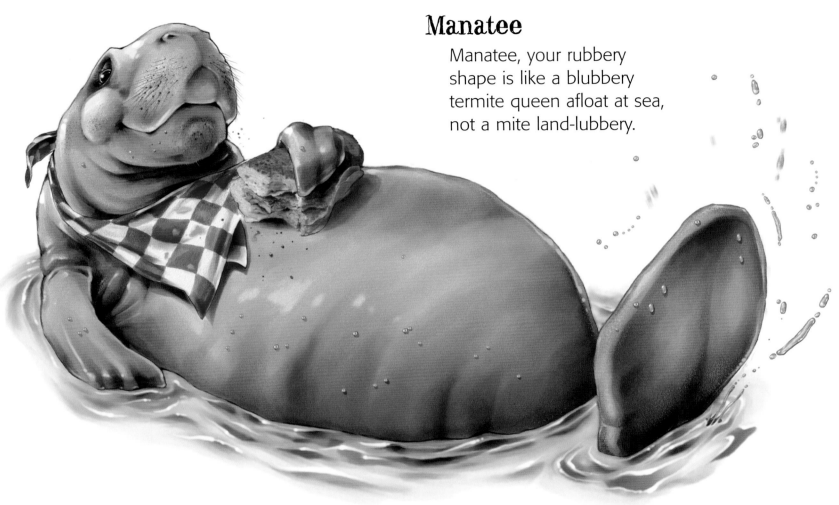

Manatee, your rubbery
shape is like a blubbery
termite queen afloat at sea,
not a mite land-lubbery.

Baby Spiders

Baby spiders
look like
BBs.

They give
people
heebie-jeebies.

Boing!

Grasshopper
leaping
on the lawn,
      hop,
   hop
like popcorn.

He's enjoying
where he's going—

        BOING!

Slow Sloth Thoughts

Oh, why do people hasten so?
I much prefer to plod
or hang
   for days
      or months
        on end
just gazing at a clod.

I contemplate the butterflies
and bugs and slugs and sod.
Oh, *why* do people hasten so?
I find it very odd.

Bad Decision

A bull saw something red.
He gored it.

It was a fire engine.
He should have
ignored it.

Teacher

Dolores knows a thing or two:
to lap up water and to chew
her doggy chow and jerky snack
without a fork. She has the knack
of eating meals utensil-free.
She knows how. She's teaching me.

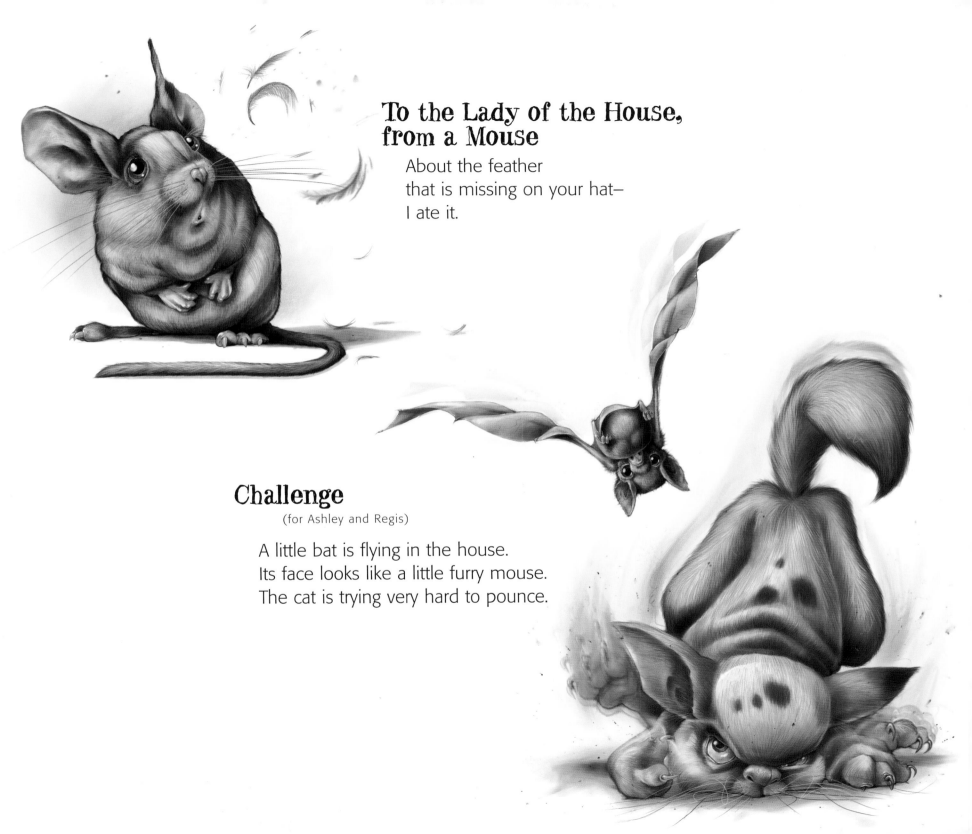

To the Lady of the House, from a Mouse

About the feather
that is missing on your hat—
I ate it.

Challenge
(for Ashley and Regis)

A little bat is flying in the house.
Its face looks like a little furry mouse.
The cat is trying very hard to pounce.

Alarm Clock

At dawn
my alarm clock struts
down the path,
hops up
onto the fence,
takes a stance
on its tough yellow feet,
gives a cough
and goes off—
COCK-A-DOODLE-DOO!

Easter Hunt

I found some chocolate eggs—exactly ten.
Now where's the chocolate hen that's laying them?

My Favorite Month

My favorite month is April, named for apes—
gorillas and orangutans who traipse
green jungles, twirling in bombastic capes
in April, the great month that's named for apes.

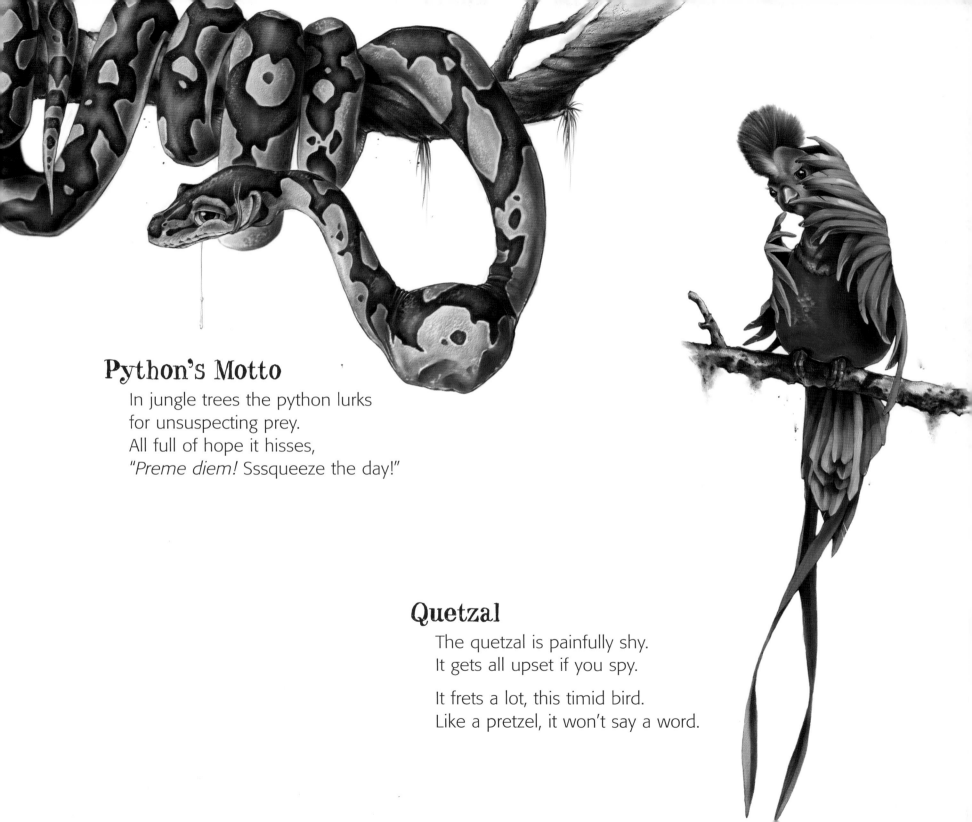

Python's Motto

In jungle trees the python lurks
for unsuspecting prey.
All full of hope it hisses,
"*Preme diem!* Sssqueeze the day!"

Quetzal

The quetzal is painfully shy.
It gets all upset if you spy.

It frets a lot, this timid bird.
Like a pretzel, it won't say a word.

Desert Dwellers

It takes practice
to
        side-
           step

cactus.

Slick Lizard

It's slick
how quick
a lizard is.

One flick
(tongue trick)
—all bugs are his.

Have You Seen a Javelina?

Have you seen a javelina?
Like a coconut of sorts.
But a coconut is quiet,
and a javelina snorts.

Vinegarroon

Vinegarrette, Vinegarroon,
grab your guitar, strum me a tune
sweet as the sage. (Strum with a prune.)

Vinegarroon, Vinegarrette,
with clever claws, clack castanet.
Click 'til the sun shows off its set.

Vinegarrette, Vinegarroon,
we'll minuet over a dune.
(In my long hair, I'll wear a spoon.)

My Vinegarrette, my Vinegarroon.

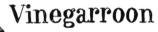

Perfect Size

The bandicoot's a big galloot—
for a rat, is what I mean.
It's not too large for a cowboy boot.
(But *way* small for a queen.)

In size, I guess it's absolute-
ly ideal for a bandicoot.

Snack Poem

A writer was writing about a goat.
A goat strolled in and ate her note-
book. (Her pen rolled down its throat.)
It leaped upon her desk to gloat.

It's no surprise, that's all she wrote.

Tony Johnston loves animals, especially odd ones. When she was ten, she tried to memorize an anthology of animal life. A bit like Will Rogers, she never met an animal she didn't like—including the diamondback. (She doesn't want one lolling on her front porch, though.) Mrs. Johnston has published more than a hundred books for young readers and has won numerous awards for her work. She lives in California.

Trip Park grew up in a veritable zoo of a home, so it seemed fitting that he illustrate *Gopher Up Your Sleeve*. As a kid, Trip rescued or revived every kind of pet from raccoons to lizards to piranhas, giving him an original take on animal anthropomorphism. A journalism graduate of the University of North Carolina at Chapel Hill, Trip was drawn to advertising as an art director, long before he began illustrating. Trip now resides in Charlotte, North Carolina with his wife, Laura, where he passes on his fascination with the animal kingdom to his own three little "wild things."

DATE DUE

MAY 23 2003			
JUN 12 2003			
JUN 20 2003			
APR 27 2004			
AUG 2 5 2004			
SEP 1 2004			

Demco, Inc. 38-293